BUTTERCUP STRIKES BACK

The city of Townsville, or whatever. One day I was in tae kwon do class, practicing my roundhouse kicks. Tae kwon do is the best – a class where you're supposed to kick and punch. Too bad school can't be more like that.

Suddenly, I heard a beeping sound. My Powerpuff pager! Someone was trying to get in touch with me. Someone who was interrupting my tae kwon do class! This had better be important, or this someone was gonna pay!

I took out my beeper and read the message. There were just two little words, but they said it all: "HELP! MOJO!"

Mojo?! This was important! Mojo Jojo is the lowest of the low. He's an evil supergenius monkey who's always making trouble for Townsville.

I really hated to leave tae kwon do early. But I knew Townsville needed me. My sisters were both off doing something dopey, so it looked like it was up to me. Besides, maybe I would get to do some real fighting against Mojo - and real fighting is even better than class!

I zoomed outside. Suddenly, I heard a kung-fu-style yell. "Hiiii-yaaa!"

I whipped around. There was Mojo Jojo. He was busting out with all kinds of kung fu moves.

You wouldn't think an evil fuzz-ball like Mojo would have the concentration and the focus to master a martial art like kung fu. But there was no time to think about that. Kung-Fu-Mojo was heading toward me. His arms and legs were a blur of chops and kicks. I might have been impressed – if I weren't so disgusted, that is.

Mojo definitely knew his chops. But I was ready for him. I flew back at the mangy monkey, using my best moves. I was prepared to pulverize him into a pile of primate powder.

MEANWHILE, THE *REAL* MOJO JOJO WAS WATCHING THE WHOLE THING FROM HIS ROBO-CAM MONITOR.

"Ha-ha-ha!" he cackled. "My plan is working! My scheme is succeeding. Take that, Powerpuff Girl Buttercup! You are no match for my specially designed Kung-Fu-Mini-Mojo-Robo. You will never defeat my mechanical Kung-Fu-Mini-Mojo. That is because my robotic fighting Mini-Mojo was not designed to be defeated. It was designed to fight forever and never give up! You, Powerpuff Girl Buttercup, will be kept busy fighting forever, so that I, Mojo Jojo, can carry out the rest of my evil plan to take over Townsville!"

7

"Maybe you should have tried talking to him first, Buttercup. You could have sung Kung-Fu-Mojo a pretty song, and then you wouldn't have had to fight."

I was getting exhausted. I was fighting my heart out, but that slimy simian hadn't even slowed down! What was up with that?

I went at him harder than ever. He punched, I kicked. He kicked, I punched. I was using all the best kung fu moves I knew. But nothing seemed to work. This guy was like a machine!

All of a sudden, I began to notice something peculiar. The whole time we were fighting, Mojo's eyes never seemed to focus on me. What kind of fighter doesn't even concentrate on his opponent?

And another thing – this Mojo didn't talk! The Mojo Jojo I know is always ranting and jabbering about how he's going to defeat The Powerpuff Girls, blah, blah, blah. But all this Mojo seemed to know was a few kung fu yells.

I flew in for a closer look. That's when I realized – this wasn't Mojo Jojo at all! It was a clever copy – a fake! This guy was nothing more than a kung fu robot!

Well, once I knew I was fighting a robot, that changed everything. I dropped the kung fu moves right away. I figured what this Mini-Mojo-Robo needed was one good power-sock in the gut. So that's exactly what I gave him. *Pow!* Special delivery! Soon that Mini-Mojo-Robo was spilling his guts all over the sidewalk.

Then the real Mojo's voice came out of a speaker. "Drat you, Powerpuff Girl Buttercup! You have ruined my robot! But you still cannot stop me from taking over Townsville! Soon all of Townsville will be mine. And you will never be able to get into City Hall to stop me!"

Naturally, I headed straight for City Hall. If Mojo Jojo thought he was going to get away with this, he had another thing coming!

When I got there, it was surrounded by an army of Mini-Mojo-Robos. I knew I was going to have to fight my way through them. I zoomed down and started punching every piece of metal I could find. I may have socked some parked cars while I was at it, but what's the big deal about a few dented fenders when there's an evil supergenius monkey trying to take over the city?

The robot guards kept coming at me, but I didn't give up. I punched them so hard that their rivets popped and their bolts came unscrewed. I tied their mechanical arms in knots. I used my eye beams to melt their silver feet together. I dented and bashed them so bad that when I was done, they weren't good for guarding anything but a junk pile.

12

I zoomed up the outside of City Hall and crashed through a window – straight into the Mayor's office.

Mojo was there, and he had taken over everything. It was a disgusting sight.

The Mayor was there, and I could see that I hadn't come a moment too soon. He was totally helpless on his own.

Bubbles was there, too. That big baby had been taken prisoner by Mojo – no surprise there, I guess. And then Blossom arrived – just popped out of an air-conditioning vent. Figures she'd try to muscle in and grab some of the attention for herself.

But there was no time for talking. . . .

It was time to fight!

"Take that, Mojo!" I yelled, flying straight at him.

My arms were like windmills. My legs were like jackhammers. I punched Mojo. I pummeled him. I kicked him and clobbered him. I threw him up in the air. I stomped on him on the ground. Blossom and Bubbles even joined in and helped a little.

By the time we were done, that chump chimp didn't know what had hit him. He was more bruised than a rotten banana.

I felt great. It had been a day full of really fun fights. In fact, I felt kind of sorry to see it all end. But I guess I could always go back to tae kwon do. . . .